I FEEL A BIT WEAK, GETAFIX ...
NO, OBELIX! YOU ARE NOT HAVING ANY MAGIC POTION! YOU KNOW VERY WELL YOU FELL INTO THE CAULDRON WHEN YOU WERE A BABY, AND IT HAD A PERMANENT EFFECT ON YOU!

GOSCINNY AND UDERZO
PRESENT
An Asterix Adventure

ASTERIX
AND THE
GREAT CROSSING

Written by RENÉ GOSCINNY *and Illustrated by* ALBERT UDERZO

Translated by Anthea Bell *and* Derek Hockridge

ORION

© 1975 GOSCINNY/UDERZO
Revised edition and English translation © 2004 HACHETTE

Original title: *La Grande traversée*

Exclusive Licensee: Orion Publishing Group
Translators: Anthea Bell and Derek Hockridge
Typography: Bryony Newhouse

This revised edition first published in 2004 by
Orion Books Ltd
Orion House, 5 Upper St Martin's Lane
London WC2H 9EA

Printed in France by Partenaires

http://gb.asterix.com
www.orionbooks.co.uk

A CIP catalogue record for this book is available from the British Library

ISBN 0752866478 (cased)
ISBN 0752866486 (paperback)

Distributed in the United States of America by Sterling Publishing Co. Inc.
387 Park Avenue South, New York, NY 10016

BELGICA

GAULISH VILLAGE

COMPENDIUM

LAUDANUM

AQUARIUM

TOTORUM

ARMORICA

LUTETIA

GAUL
(ROMAN CONQUEST)
50 BC

CELTICA

AQUITANIA

PROVINCIA

THE YEAR IS 50 BC. GAUL IS ENTIRELY OCCUPIED BY THE
ROMANS. WELL, NOT ENTIRELY ... ONE SMALL VILLAGE OF
INDOMITABLE GAULS STILL HOLDS OUT AGAINST THE INVADERS.
AND LIFE IS NOT EASY FOR THE ROMAN LEGIONARIES WHO
GARRISON THE FORTIFIED CAMPS OF TOTORUM, AQUARIUM,
LAUDANUM AND COMPENDIUM ...

ASTERIX, THE HERO OF THESE ADVENTURES. A SHREWD, CUNNING LITTLE WARRIOR, ALL PERILOUS MISSIONS ARE IMMEDIATELY ENTRUSTED TO HIM. ASTERIX GETS HIS SUPERHUMAN STRENGTH FROM THE MAGIC POTION BREWED BY THE DRUID GETAFIX . . .

OBELIX, ASTERIX'S INSEPARABLE FRIEND. A MENHIR DELIVERY MAN BY TRADE, ADDICTED TO WILD BOAR. OBELIX IS ALWAYS READY TO DROP EVERYTHING AND GO OFF ON A NEW ADVENTURE WITH ASTERIX – SO LONG AS THERE'S WILD BOAR TO EAT, AND PLENTY OF FIGHTING. HIS CONSTANT COMPANION IS DOGMATIX, THE ONLY KNOWN CANINE ECOLOGIST, WHO HOWLS WITH DESPAIR WHEN A TREE IS CUT DOWN.

GETAFIX, THE VENERABLE VILLAGE DRUID, GATHERS MISTLETOE AND BREWS MAGIC POTIONS. HIS SPECIALITY IS THE POTION WHICH GIVES THE DRINKER SUPERHUMAN STRENGTH. BUT GETAFIX ALSO HAS OTHER RECIPES UP HIS SLEEVE . . .

CACOFONIX, THE BARD. OPINION IS DIVIDED AS TO HIS MUSICAL GIFTS. CACOFONIX THINKS HE'S A GENIUS. EVERY-ONE ELSE THINKS HE'S UNSPEAKABLE. BUT SO LONG AS HE DOESN'T SPEAK, LET ALONE SING, EVERYBODY LIKES HIM . . .

FINALLY, VITALSTATISTIX, THE CHIEF OF THE TRIBE. MAJESTIC, BRAVE AND HOT-TEMPERED, THE OLD WARRIOR IS RESPECTED BY HIS MEN AND FEARED BY HIS ENEMIES. VITALSTATISTIX HIMSELF HAS ONLY ONE FEAR, HE IS AFRAID THE SKY MAY FALL ON HIS HEAD TOMORROW. BUT AS HE ALWAYS SAYS, TOMORROW NEVER COMES.

WØØF! WØØF!

DØWN, HUNTINGSEÅSSEN! GØ TØ BYE-BYES, LITTLE DØGGY!

FUNNY SØRT ØF IDEÅ, TÅKING THÅT DØG ÅLØNG! FUNNY SØRT ØF IDEÅ TÅKING THIS VØYÅGE ÅNYWÅY! YØU'RE Å VISIØNÅRY, HERENDETHELESSEN!

YØU WÅIT ÅND SEE! YØU'LL ÅLL FIND ØUT I'M RIGHT! ÅND NØW SHUT UP!

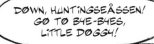

ER... HERENDETHELESSEN... WØULD THÅT WHITE THING ØVER TØ STÅRBØÅRD BE ÅN ICEBERG, BY ÅNY CHÅNCE?

ØVER TØ PØRT JUST Å WHISKER!

I SEE...

(BUT LET US LEAVE THESE ICY SEAS, VEILED IN DENSE, IMPENETRABLE MISTS...)

①

...AND MAKE FOR A LITTLE GAULISH VILLAGE BASKING IN THE SUN.

THIS IS THE LIMIT!

THE ABSOLUTE LIMIT!

UNHYGIENIX FISHMONGER

MY TWO SHIELD-BEARERS ATE SOME OF YOUR FISH YESTERDAY, AND NOW THEY'RE WRITHING IN AGONY, HALF POISONED! AND I HAVE TO DO THEIR WORK FOR THEM!

I'M AFRAID THIS IS THE END OF MY STOCK...

I WAS EXPECTING A DELIVERY, BUT THE OX CARTS BRINGING FISH FROM LUTETIA ARE ON STRIKE. THEY'RE GOING SLOW ALONG THE ROMAN ROADS IN PROTEST AGAINST THE PRICE OF HAY.

7

BLOiNG! BANG!

ISN'T IT NICE WHEN THEY FIGHT EACH OTHER?

DEAD RIGHT IT IS!

HOWEVER, IRA FUROR BREVIS EST, AS I ALWAYS SAY, SO DON'T LET'S HANG AROUND!

THE DECURION IS CORRECT; ANGER IS A BRIEF MADNESS...

I ASK YOU! THE MOMENT I START, THEY ALL STOP! SULKING IS A BAD HABIT.

ANYWAY, WHY HAVEN'T YOU GOT ANY FRESH FISH?

OH, DON'T START THAT ALL OVER AGAIN! I'VE ALREADY TOLD YOU, I WAS EXPECTING A DELIVERY!

BUT THERE'S THE SEA, RIGHT NEXT TO THIS VILLAGE.

THE SEA? WHAT'S THE SEA GOT TO DO WITH MY FISH?

ALL YOU HAVE TO DO IS GO FISHING FOR FISH IN THE SEA.

LET ME TELL YOU, MY GOOD SIR, I SELL TOP QUALITY FISH FROM LUTETIA! MY CUSTOMERS TRUST ME!

I GET MY FISH FROM THE BEST WHOLESALERS! I'M NOT SELLING ANY OLD FISH JUST OUT OF THE WATER! YOU NEVER KNOW WHERE THEY'VE BEEN!

IF YOU WANT FRESH FISH YOU'LL HAVE TO WAIT FOR IT!

UNHYGIEN

NO.

TCHRRRRRiiiiK!

?

NO, I CAN'T WAIT.

UNHYGIEI... FISHMON...

I NEED A BIT OF REASONABLY FRESH FISH TO MAKE MY MAGIC POTION. THERE'S HARDLY ANY LEFT.

SO IN THE INTERESTS OF SECURITY, SOMEONE HAS TO GO FISHING.

WE'LL GO FISHING.

OOH YES, WE'LL GO, WON'T WE DOGMATIX?

I FELT SURE YOU WOULD, BOYS!

MY FISHING BOAT'S ON THE BEACH. THE ONE I USED TO USE AS A BOY.

YOU OUGHT TO WAIT FOR A BRIGHT PERIOD... I DON'T LIKE THE LOOK OF THE SKY!

OH, WELL, SO LONG AS IT DOESN'T FALL ON OUR HEADS!

TAKE A DROP OF MAGIC POTION. YOU NEVER KNOW!

IS THAT REALLY NECESSARY? WE'RE NOT GOING FAR, AND THERE'S NO ONE ELSE OUT THERE.

MAY BELENOS PROTECT YOU!

9

THROW OUT THE NET, OBELIX!

AYE, AYE, SIR!

HOW DO WE GET THE NET BACK NOW?

JUST PULL IT IN.

PULL IT IN? BUT I'VE THROWN IT OUT!

YOU MEAN TO SAY YOU DIDN'T TIE IT TO SOMETHING FIRST?

YOU MUST BE CRAZY, THROWING A NET OUT LIKE THAT!

YOU TOLD ME TO THROW IT OUT, SO I DID THROW IT OUT!

I'M A MENHIR DELIVERY-MAN, I AM! NOT A FISHERMAN!

ALL RIGHT, CALM DOWN. WE'LL JUST HAVE TO GO BACK FOR ANOTHER NET!

THE WIND'S TOO STRONG! WE CAN'T GO ABOUT!

HUH! HE LAUGHS AT ME AND HE CAN'T EVEN SAIL A BOAT!

I DON'T NEED ANY MENHIR DELIVERY-MEN GIVING ME ADVICE!

YOU SEE? WE HAVEN'T COME TO THE EDGE OF THE SEA, THERE AREN'T ANY MONSTERS, AND THE WIND'S DIED DOWN.

WE CAN'T SEE LAND ANY MORE...

WE'LL TURN BACK HOME AS SOON AS WE GET A FAVOURABLE BREEZE. WE'VE JUST GOT TO WAIT.

8A

I'M HUNGRY!

THINK OF SOMETHING ELSE.

IF YOU HADN'T TOLD ME TO THROW OUT THE NET, WE COULD HAVE CAUGHT SOME FISH... I'D RATHER EAT A BOAR, OF COURSE.

I SAID THINK OF SOMETHING ELSE... THINK OF YOUR MENHIRS.

WITH THAT SAUCE IMPEDIMENTA MAKES, I COULD EAT A MENHIR... REMEMBER THAT SAUCE?

MMM, YES!... VERY GOOD, SPECIALLY WHEN SHE PUTS IN THOSE LITTLE ONIONS AND BITS OF BACON...

ASTERIX! I'M HUNGRY!

I'M HUNGRY TOO! IT'S YOU MAKING ME HUNGRY, GOING ON ABOUT MENHIRS WITH ONIONS!

?

LOOK!

A SHIP!

8B

THERE'S A SIGHT FOR SORE EYES, MY BOY!

IT'S VERY NICE OF YOU TO THINK OF CELEBRATING MY BIRTHDAY!

DONEC ERIS FELIX, MULTOS NUMERABIS AMICOS.

WHY DON'T YOU STOP MAKING SILLY REMARKS AND COME ON DECK TO SUMMON THE CREW INSTEAD? THEN WE'LL START THE PARTY!

SAIL ON THE STARBOARD TACK!

OH, NEVER MIND WHAT TACK SHE'S ON! WE'RE OFF THE HARD TACK FOR ONCE. COME ON, TUCK IN, ME HEARTIES!

HELP! LOOK! THAT REALLY TAKES THE BISCUIT! IT'S THEM!

THEY'RE NOT BOTHERING TO STOP!

COME ON, WE'LL CATCH THEM UP. THERE'S NO WIND, SO YOU'LL HAVE TO PUSH.

YUM, YUM!

WE MUST RATION OURSELVES. I THINK THE STORM BLEW US A LONG WAY FROM HOME.

OH, VERY WELL!

SOON AFTERWARDS...

OBELIX! YOU REALLY ARE THE LIMIT! I TOLD YOU WE SHOULD RATION OURSELVES!

WELL, I HAVE...

I'VE KEPT THIS FOR LATER...

OH, PERHAPS YOU'RE RIGHT... NOW WE'VE EATEN LET'S HAVE A LITTLE SNOOZE.

MAYBE YOU WERE WRONG TO LEAVE THEM THE SAUSAGE.

GO TO SLEEP!

BRAOUMMM!

CRACK!

THIS STORM IS BLOWING US STILL FARTHER FROM HOME! IT'S DRIVING US TOWARDS THE SETTING SUN!

I JUST FEEL LIKE AN APPLE NOW!

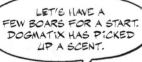

17

18

THERE AREN'T ANY BEARS NEAR OUR VILLAGE ... SO WHERE ARE WE?

I'M TRYING TO DISCOVER, THE SAME AS YOU.

SNIFF!

WELL, WE'LL EAT THIS BEAR AND AFTER THAT, BY TOUTATIS, WE'LL SEE!

DON'T YOU WANT ANY? THERE'S STILL A BIT LEFT...

NO... I'M WONDERING WHERE WE CAN HAVE FETCHED UP...

SCRUNCH!

A LITTLE LATER...

OH, WELL, LET'S HAVE A REST... WE'LL SEE LATER.

GOOD IDEA!

DOGMATIX HAS PICKED UP ANOTHER SCENT!

OH, GOODY, SOMETHING ELSE TO EAT! I REALLY AM RAVENOUS.

GRRRRRR!

RAVENOUS? YOU'VE ONLY JUST EATEN TWO GOBBLERS, ONE OF THEM STUFFED WITH BEAR.

IT'LL TAKE A LOT OF GOBBLERS AND A LOT OF BEARS TO MAKE ME FORGET THAT APPLE!

ASTERIX! COME AND LOOK! ROMANS!

?

15

WHERE?

HERE!

THEY MAY NOT BE ROMANS.

OF COURSE THEY ARE! JUST LIKE ROMANS TO BE OUT IN THE FOREST SPYING ON US, TOO FRIGHTENED TO SHOW THEIR FACES.

LET'S GO AND LOOK FOR THEM. IF WE CATCH ANY THEY CAN TELL US THE WAY TO THE VILLAGE.

ALL RIGHT, BUT TREAD VERY QUIETLY. YOU NEVER KNOW...

YOOHOO! ROMANS! WHERE ARE YOU, ROMANS?

SSH! I TOLD YOU TO TREAD QUIETLY!

I AM TREADING QUIETLY, I'M NOT MAKING A BIT OF NOISE WITH MY FEET!

WON'T YOU EVER UNDERSTAND ANYTHING?

WELL, SO WHO TOLD ME TO THROW OUT THE NET?!

WHAT'S THE NET GOT TO DO WITH THIS?

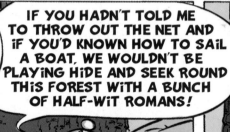

IF YOU HADN'T TOLD ME TO THROW OUT THE NET AND IF YOU'D KNOWN HOW TO SAIL A BOAT, WE WOULDN'T BE PLAYING HIDE AND SEEK ROUND THIS FOREST WITH A BUNCH OF HALF-WIT ROMANS!

BOING!

YES, WELL, OUR ROMANS CAN'T BE FAR AWAY. LET'S TRY TO FIND THEM.

BUT HOW?

WE ONLY HAVE TO FOLLOW THE ARROW IN THE OPPOSITE DIRECTION FROM THE WAY IT'S POINTING. THAT'S LOGICAL.

THAT'S LOGICAL?

20

I'M GOING TO TEACH YOU A HUNTSMAN'S TRICK! YOU IMITATE THE CRY OF YOUR QUARRY. LISTEN!

GOBBLE GOBBLE GOBBLE! GOBBLE!

GOBBLE GOBBLE GOBBLE

OVER IN THAT TREE... OF COURSE, THOSE GOBBLERS ARE BIRDS, SO THEY MUST HAVE NESTS. THAT'S THE DIFFERENCE BETWEEN GOBBLERS AND BOARS.

YES, I CAN SEE ITS FEATHERS! NOW TO GET HOLD OF IT!

TWEET, TWEET, TWEET...

?!

KERPLONK!

IT'S A ROMAN DISGUISED AS A GOBBLER... WE CAN'T EAT HIM, BUT HE CAN TELL US THE WAY TO THE VILLAGE!

LOOK, ASTERIX! JULIUS CAESAR HAS STARTED DISGUISING HIS LEGIONARIES AS GOBBLERS! THESE ROMANS ARE...

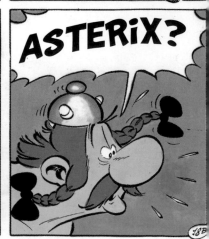

ASTERIX?

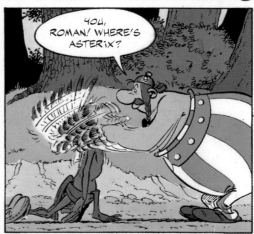

UGH?

I THINK HE WANTS TO KNOW WHO WE ARE.

DOES HE, THOUGH!

WE ARE GAULS, AND THIS IS OUR NATIVE LAND! SO CRETANS GO HOME TO CRETE, AND DON'T BE CRETINS! YOU'LL NEVER CONQUER US!!!

?

HE DIDN'T UNDERSTAND. GET ME UNTIED AND WE'LL DO IT IN MIME FOR HIM.

WE ARE BRAVE...

WE HAVE ONLY ONE FEAR: THAT THE SKY MAY FALL ON OUR HEADS...

WE LIKE A BIT OF A JOKE!

WE LIKE OUR FOOD AND DRINK...

SOMETIMES WE LOSE OUR TEMPERS...

GRRRR!

POO!

WE ARE A ROWDY LOT AND WE LIKE A PUNCH-UP...

BONK-BONK!

GRRR! GRRR!

...BUT WE LOVE OUR FRIENDS!

IN SHORT...

WE ARE GAULS!

HE GETS THE IDEA!

TAP TAP TAP!

I THINK HE'S CHALLENGING YOU!

YOU DO?

GLUG! GLUG!

PAF!

I'VE FINISHED MINE.

MY TURN, THEN.

PAFFF!

HOHOHOHO HOHOHOHO

SOON AFTERWARDS...

I THINK HE WANTS US TO STAY HERE.

LOOK, I'M NOT JOINING UP IN THE ROMAN ARMY!

WELL, LET'S ACCEPT. THAT WAY WE MAY FINALLY FIND OUT WHERE WE ARE.

27

A LITTLE LATER...

LET HIM. IT MUST MEAN WE'VE BEEN TAKEN ON AS RECRUITS.

WHO'D HAVE THOUGHT I'D EVER WEAR THE UNIFORM OF A ROMAN MERCENARY?

HAVE YOU NOTICED THE LITTLE CRETAN GIRLS? I WOULDN'T MIND BEING IN THIS CRETE WITH A FEW LIKE THAT...

WELL, DON'T GO BEING INDISCREET HERE.

GOBBLEGOBBLE?

WOOF WOOF.

SLAP!

SCRUNCH!

28

NEXT MORNING..

I THINK HE'S INVITING US TO GO HUNTING.

GOOD! NOW I'LL KNOW WE WON'T BE EATING HOT DOG!

DO YOU THINK WE SHOULD BE DOING THE SAME AS THEM?

I THINK WE SHOULD...

TOM! TOM! TOM!

TOM! TOM!

I'VE GOT IT! I SEE NOW! THEY'RE IBERIANS! IBERIANS LOVE DANCING!

OLÉ! OLÉ!

CLACK! CLACK!

SSSSH, OBELIX!

?

OLÉ! OLÉ! OLÉ!

SEE?

?

OLÉ! OLÉ!

I'D LIKE TO KEEP THIS AS A SOUVENIR OF OUR DAY'S HUNTING...

ESPECIALLY AS THE IBERIANS SEEMED QUITE IMPRESSED WITH OUR TECHNIQUE!

UGH!

OH, HOW KIND!

?

AHU!

??

GRRRR

I THINK IT'S HIS DAUGHTER, AND HE'S PLEASED SHE LIKES YOU.

WHAT?

BONK.

HEY, THIS FAT IBERIAN GIRL IS FOLLOWING ME AROUND!

UGH!

TEEHEEHEE!
?

OLÉ!

WHAT DOES THAT CENTURION WANT ME TO DO?
I THINK HE WANTS YOU TO MARRY HIS DAUGHTER!

NO, THANK YOU VERY MUCH! I DON'T WANT TO BE A CENTURION'S SON-IN-LAW!

ANYWAY, I'M TOO YOUNG!
I THINK THE TIME HAS COME FOR US TO START LOOKING FOR OUR VILLAGE AGAIN... I'VE AN IDEA WE'RE A LONG WAY FROM HOME.

WHILE WE WERE HUNTING, I NOTICED THAT WE'RE ON AN ISLAND... WE'LL NEED A BOAT.
I SAW SOME BOATS DOWN BY THE RIVER.

GOOD. TONIGHT WE'LL TRY TO WELSH ON OUR HOSTS!
TWO WELSH? WHAT, WITH ALL THESE CRETANS AND IBERIANS AROUND THE PLACE ALREADY?

THAT NIGHT...

CRACK!

HE'S HEARD US!

HANG ON!

GOBBLE GOBBLE GOBBLE GOBBLE

28A

UGH!

SOON AFTERWARDS...

THAT WAS A GOOD TRICK!

I SURE HAVE LEARNT A THING OR TWO HOME ON THIS RANGE!

I'VE NEVER SEEN A BOAT LIKE THIS BEFORE!

YES, THAT HOLE TO LET THE WATER IN IS RATHER UNUSUAL.

BLOP!
BLOP!
BLOP!
BLOP!

!

28B

32

GROÔÂÂR

PAT!
PAT!
PAT!

MÅYBE HUNTINGSEÅSSEN HÅS SCENTED LÅND...

WHÅT LÅND, HERENDETHE-LESSEN?

I DØN'T BELIEVE IN THIS LÅND YOU KEEP ØN ÅBOUT! NØ ØNE BELIEVES IN IT! THERE ISN'T ÅNY LÅND! WE'RE GØING TØ COME TO THE EDGE ØF THE SEÅ ÅND THEN FÅLL ØFF, BY THØR!

YOU NEVER BELIEVE ÅNYTHING, STEPTØÅNSSEN! I'M SURE THERE'S LÅND ÅHEÅD! IT MÅY EVEN BE INHÅBITED!

I SHÅLL DISCØVER THIS LÅND, ÅND TÅKE HØME SOME ØF THE NÅTIVES TO PRØVE IT!

LET'S TURN BÅCK WHILE THERE'S STILL TIME! WHÅT DØ YOU SÅY, HÅRÅLDWILSSEN? ÅND YOU, NØGOODREÅSSEN? ÅND YOU LØT?

YERSSE!

GRØØ AÅRR!

THÅT HØUND ØF YØURS IS BEGINNING TØ...

LØØK! LØØK, BY ØDIN!

A SHIP!

ROMAN, GOTHIC, EGYPTIAN OR WHAT?

WHO CARES? THAT SHIP MAY BE ABLE TO GET US HOME!

THOSE MERCENARIES MIGHT WELL CATCH UP WITH US... AND THEY WOULDN'T BE VERY PLEASED WE GOT AWAY... SPECIALLY YOU!

HOW RIGHT YOU ARE! LET'S SIGNAL TO THEM!

3/A

SOON AFTERWARDS...

I'VE BUILT A LITTLE HEAP OF STONES... BUT DO YOU REALLY THINK...

YOU WANT TO MARRY THE CENTURION'S DAUGHTER?

NO FEAR! I VALUE MY LIBERTY!

WELL THEN...

3/B

35

LÅND! INHÅBITED, ÅT THÅT! PULL HÅRD, BØYS!

THEY'VE SEEN US! THEY'RE COMING!

CREEÅÅK!

ØNE SMÅLL STEP FØR ME, Å GIÅNT LEÅP FØR MÅNKIND!

WHÅT WÅS ÅLL THÅT ÅBØUT?

IT JUST SØRT ØF CÅME TØ ME... HÅND ME THE BEÅDS. WE'LL SØFTEN THEM UP!

WHAT'S ALL THIS JUNK IN AID OF?

THEY MUST BE DOOR-TO-DOOR SALESMEN TRYING TO FLOG THEIR STUFF.

THEY LØØK PLEÅSED... LET'S STRIKE WHILE THE IRØN'S HØT!

NÅTIVES, YØU CØME WITH US IN ØUR SHIP?

WHAT'S HE SAYING?

I'VE NO IDEA. I'LL TRY AND TALK TO HIM.

MERCHANTS, YOU TAKE US IN YOUR SHIP?

WHÅT?

LET'S TRY TO GET ÅCQUÅINTED. I'LL DO THE INTRODUCTIONS. ME HERENDETHELESSEN THE ÅDVENTUROUS...

HIM NØGØØD-REÅSSEN THE NUTCÅSE...

YEÅH!

ME STEPTØÅNSSEN SHIFTY-EYES...

ME HÅRÅLDWILSSEN THE INTELLECTUÅL. YOU WHÅT?

I THINK THEY WANT TO KNOW WHO WE ARE.

WELL, LET'S PUT ON THE SHOW WE GAVE THOSE ROMAN COLONIALS AGAIN.

34A

BONG BONG

IT'S ALL RIGHT, ASTERIX. THEY GET THE IDEA.

TÅP! TÅP! TÅP!

34B

SURE ENOUGH, IT IS A FAST CROSSING, AND SOON A THICK FOG COVERS THE ICY SEA...

LÅND!

WE'RE BÅCK! PREPÅRE TØ HÅVE HØNØURS HEÅPED UPØN YØU!

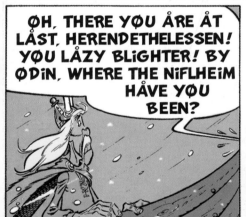

ØH, THERE YØU ÅRE ÅT LÅST, HERENDETHELESSEN! YØU LÅZY BLIGHTER! BY ØDIN, WHERE THE NIFLHEIM HÅVE YØU BEEN?

IT'S... IT'S ØDIUSCØMPÅRISSEN THE TERRIFYING, THE CHIEF ØF ØUR TRIBE!

ØF CØURSE IT'S ØDIUSCØMPÅRISSEN! DID YØU THINK IT WÅS Å DEÅR LITTLE MERMÅID?

I SÅLUTE YØU, Ø CHIEF ØDIUSCØMPÅRISSEN!

ÅND I DØN'T SÅLUTE YØU!

WHILE WE WERE ÅLL ØUT ØN Å RÅIDING EXPEDITIØN, MR HERENDETHELESSEN WENT FØR Å CRUISE!

WE HÅVE PILLÅGED ÅND BURNT, WE'VE BRØUGHT BÅCK PLUNDER, SLÅVES, WHILE YØU...

WHILE I'VE BEEN DISCØVERING Å WØRLD... Å NEW WØRLD!

41

Å WORLD?

Å NEW WORLD.

HØHØHØHØHØHØ! Å NEW WØRLD! JUST HÅRK ÅT HiM!

THÅT'S RIGHT! Å LÅND ØF ØPPØRTUNITY, ÅND ÅLL WE HÅVE TØ DØ iS CØNQUER iT!

HÅVE YØU GØT ÅNY PRØØF ØF THiS?

ÅND I DØN'T MEÅN THE BLÅTHERiNGS ØF THÅT LÅZY LØT WHØ WENT WiTH YØU!

HERE ÅRE MY PRØØFS CØMING ÅSHØRE.

EXCUSE ME, SiR, CØULD YØU PØSSIBLY HELP US? WE'RE LØØKiNG FØR Å LITTLE GÅULiSH VILLAGE WHiCH...

?

WHØ ÅRE THESE CLØWNS ÅND WHÅT ÅRE THEY SÅYiNG?

THEY'RE INHÅBITÅNTS ØF THE NEW WØRLD. UNFØRTUNÅTELY NØ ØNE CÅN UNDERSTÅND THEIR LÅNGUÅGE.

THEY DØN'T LØØK VERY EXØTiC...

SEE HØW DIFFERENT THEIR DØG iS FRØM ØURS.

THiS GAULISH VILLAGE I WAS TALKING ABØUT...

HMMM...

YØU LØT, BÅCK TØ MY PLÅCE! I WÅNT TØ HEÅR MØRE ÅBØUT THiS!

42

RIGHT, LET'S HEAR THIS SÅGÅ!

GØ ØN, HÅRÅLD-WILSSEN!

UM... ER...

FULL ØF HØPE ÅND CØURÅGE WE SET FØRTH, ØNE MISTY MØRNING IN...

CUT IT SHØRT, YØU FØØL, ØR I SHALL CUT YØU SHORT WITH THIS!

TWO MINUTES LATER...

...TILL BÅCK THIS MØRNING STOP DELIGHTED HEÅR BELOVED. CHIEF'S DULCET VØICE STOP

ÅMÅZING! ÅND DØES THIS LÅND LØØK RICH?

SEE HØW WELL-NØURISHED THIS NÅTIVE IS. ÅND THE ØTHER ØNE MÅY SEEM FRÅIL, BUT HE HÅS SUPERHUMÅN STRENGTH!

WØMEN! GERTRUDE! INTRUDE! IRMGÅRD! FIREGÅRD! GET Å FEÅST REÅDY STRÅIGHT ÅWÅY! WE'RE GØING TØ CELEBRÅTE THE RETURN ØF ØUR HERØES ÅND ØUR IMMINENT DEPÅRTURE FØR THE NEW WØRLD!

WE'LL EAT, DRiNK ÅND MÅKE MERRY ÅND HÅVE Å NiCE FiGHT!

BØNK!

YØUR NÅTiVES CÅN JØiN THE FUN TØØ! AFTERWARDS WE'LL SÅCRiFiCE THEM TØ THE GØDS. iT iS AN HØNØUR RiCHLY DESERVED!

HUH! WHÅT FØR? THEY HÅVEN'T DØNE Å THiNG!

WE ÅLL HÅVE TØ LEÅRN TØ MÅKE SÅCRiFiCES.

DON'T DRiNK TØØ MUCH.

OH, COME ON, LET'S HAVE A BiT OF FUN. i LiKE THESE PEOPLE.

WHY, YØU'RE GAULS!

?

?

WHÅT? YØU, SLÅVE! CØME HERE!

CØMiNG... i MEAN CØMiNG MÅSTER!

CÅN YØU TÅLK TØ THESE PEØPLE FROM THE NEW WØRLD?

NEW WØRLD?... BUT THEY'RE GÅULS, THE SAME AS ME... SØRRY, THE SÅME ÅS ME!

THiS SLÅVE WiTH THE ÅWFUL ÅCCENT iS LYiNG! HE MUST BE Å NÅTiVE ØF THE NEW WØRLD TØØ!

NEW WØRLD? HUH! YØU'VE BEEN SLØPiNG ØFF TØ GAUL, THÅT'S WHÅT! CHÅSiNG THE LUTETiÅN GiRLS, EH?!

THEY'VE MÅDE ØFF WITH THE SLÅVE ÅND HIS BØÅT!

YØU ØLD RÅSCÅL! TRYING TØ FØØL ME WITH YØUR TÅLES ØF Å NEW WØRLD!

BUT I FØRGIVE YØU! IT WÅS Å SPLENDID FIGHT, ÅND WE'VE HÅD Å LØT ØF FUN!
BØNK!

BUT NØ SHIRKING NEXT TIME! CØME ÅND HÅVE Å DRINK!

ÅM I SUPPØSED TØ BE Å DISCØVERER, ØR ÅM I NØT...?

CØMING, HERENDETHE-LESSEN?

TØ BE ØR NØT TØ BE, THÅT IS THE QUESTIØN...

SEVERAL DAYS LATER...

THEY'RE BACK! THEY'RE BACK!

47

THE END

48

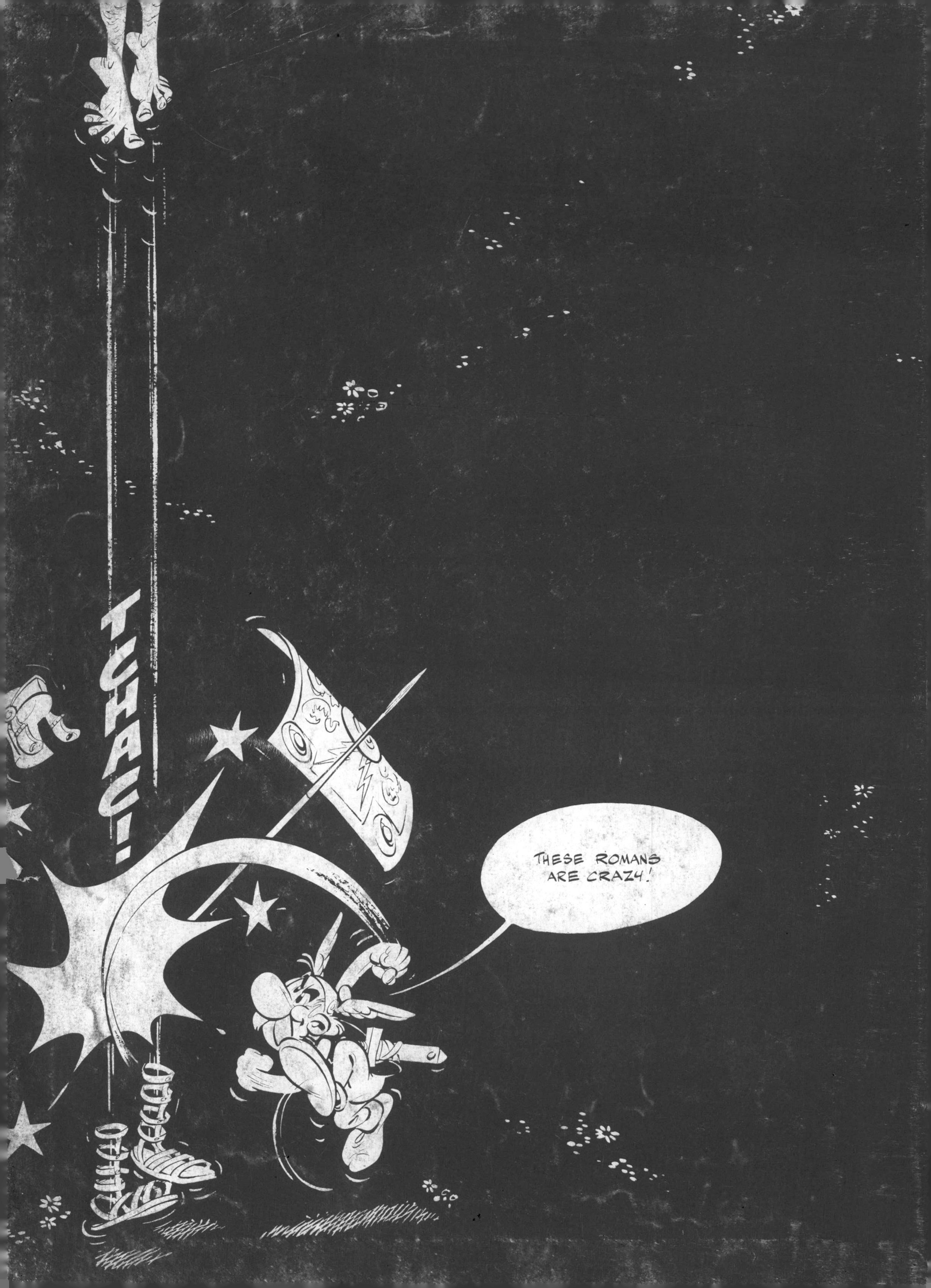
TCHAC!
THESE ROMANS ARE CRAZY!